D1416461

OCT   2012

I HATE BULLIES!

Copyright © 2005 by Hans Wilhelm, Inc.

All rights reserved. Published by Scholastic Inc.
SCHOLASTIC, CARTWHEEL BOOKS, NOODLES, and associated logos
are trademarks and/or registered trademarks of Scholastic Inc.
Lexile is a registered trademark of MetaMetrics, Inc.

Library of Congress Cataloging-in-Publication Data is available.

ISBN 978-0-439-70139-6

12 11 10 9 8 7 6 5 4 3   10 11 12 13 14 15/0

Printed in the U.S.A   40

This edition first printing, July 2011

SCHOLASTIC READER
LEVEL 1
50-250 WORDS

I HATE BULLIES!

by Hans Wilhelm

Cartwheel
·B·O·O·K·S·®

SCHOLASTIC INC.

New York   Toronto   London   Auckland
Sydney   Mexico City   New Delhi   Hong Kong

Look what I have.

Go away! This is MY bone.

HELP!

I am safe.

It's good to be small.

Oh, no!
The gate is open.

Let go of my bone!

I hate bullies.

This is not fair.

I have an idea!

Turn on the hose.

Here we go!

Run, Bully, run!

I got my bone back.

I will eat it inside.